THE COUNTRY EARTHLING: I FINALLY GOT A BOY!
Copyright © 2024 by FALISHIA WALKER
ISBN: 979-8-9901529-0-8
Library of Congress Control Number is on file.
Published in Austin, Texas

The Country Earthling

Vol.1

I Finally Got a Boy!

Written by: FaLishia Walker

Illustrated by: Autumn Taylor

I am Iggy the Piggy and this is Hiram, my human best friend.

Hiram's dad said that my boy can live in the backyard with me.

We really like it out here!

His dad wants us to love fruits and vegetables. But we love pizza, chips, and lollipops more.

We are both 5. I will live to be 50 years old. My boy, Hiram can live longer than me.

I am independent at 4 weeks old. Hiram has to stay with his dad until he is a young adult.

Hiram and I are both mammals. Mammals have hair on them.

I am a potbelly pig!

Hiram is a mammal.

He is a human boy!

Hiram is my best friend!

We do everything together!
We run, we laugh, we
pretend, and chase his
sister all day! What a life!

Hiram, The Monster!

Sister, The spicy spy!

Piggy, the water pig!

17

Sometimes when it is hot outside, Hiram's dad lets us play in the mud. We have lots of fun, until...

...bedtime!

When it is time for bed the fun stops but that is okay.

We are just a day away until the fun starts over again!

Sight Words

can	I
has	A
laugh	do
all	fun
run	know

Sight Words

have	to
pig	we
live	in
that	my
can	and

Potbelly Pig Facts

Did you know....

1. Potbellied pigs came from Southeast Asia in the 1980's and were imported to the United States as pets. It is formally known as a Vietnamese Lon 1. It is black and has short legs and a low hanging belly.

2. Potbellied pigs have sensitive skin and they will get sunburned just like we do!

3. Potbellied pigs are smart and are very trainable. They can be taught to do tricks and respond to commands, just like dogs!

4. Potbellied pigs use their noses for more than just smelling. Their snouts are strong and they use them to push things around.

5. A potbellied pig can grow to be between 80 and 180 pounds.

6. Potbellied pigs are friendly and social animals.

7. Potbellied pigs have bad eyesight, but they have a great sense of smell and have exceptional hearing.

8. Potbellied pigs can get overweight and if this happens it can actually cause "mechanical blindness". This is where rolls of fat obscure their eyesight, but it can be reversed with diet and exercise.

9. Potbellied pigs are surprisingly quick and enjoy running. They can also swim in shallow water.

10. Potbellied pigs only sweat a little bit on their nose and nowhere else. For this reason, they stick to the shade and enjoy cooling off in the mud. Mud also protects their skin, so it's a win-win!

Click on the QR code below and enjoy small surprises from the book.

Like, share, and subscribe to "The Country Earthling"

Meet the Author

FaLishia Walker

FaLishia Walker wants kids to enjoy reading. Learning about animals is an excellent way to build vocabulary and sight words. Guess what, you get the sight words at the back of each book!

FaLishia Walker has always been a reader. She has always been business-minded. Her first "business" was renting her library books for $0.25 outside of her bedroom window, at the age of 8; in Willis, Texas. She is not so much of an animal lover as she is a lover of reading.

She is an Army Reserve Veteran, committed to being a lifelong Educator, and a business owner.

"I want to do this animal series with Autumn Taylor, my Illustrator and my cousin. Why not make it a family affair? She's talented and ambitious; and the world of books needs her contribution."

Meet the Illustrator

Autumn Taylor

Autumn Taylor is a student of the art. She enjoys learning and creating different art styles and techniques.

"I aim to connect with my audience and to spark meaningful conversations about my masterpiece(s)."

At the age of four, due to boredom, her art journey began. Drawing household items and recreating art pieces occupied her time. By the time she was in 9th grade, she won Special Merit at the Houston Rodeo and was selected as a top contender. She was chosen 42nd out of 1,000 contestants that had entered. In the 12th Grade, she won Grand Champion at Aldine FFA Art Show in 2018.

She is currently pursuing her degree in Communication and Design at the University of Houston-Victoria.

105 Publishing LLC
Austin, TX
www.105publishing.com

Made in the USA
Columbia, SC
09 July 2024